T⊛XIC

" When they emerged from the wood they found themselves on a narrow track. It ended when they reached the high wooden perimeter fence.

'That's pretty good for stopping anyone getting into the camp,' mused Arjun, staring up at the fence.

'Maybe it's to stop us getting out!' grinned Kev, doing his best 'deranged monster attack' impression. **"**

ZOMBIE CAMP

Zombie Camp
by Jonny Zucker
Illustrated by Stuart Harrison

Published by Ransom Publishing Ltd.
Radley House, 8 St. Cross Road, Winchester, Hampshire
SO23 9HX, UK
www.ransom.co.uk

ISBN   978 178127 718 8
First published in 2015

ZOMBIE CAMP

JONNY ZUCKER

ILLUSTRATED BY
STUART HARRISON

Ransom

CHAPTER 1

Arjun dived for the ball and caught it.

'Excellent catch!' shouted Marcus. 'Kev, you're batting next.'

Kev grabbed the bat off the floor and prepared for his first strike.

Arjun Taur and Kev Lane were standing in a large, freshly-mowed field with a bunch of kids their age. The sky was a tranquil blue; a bright sun shone down on them, delivering delicious summer heat.

They were on a summer sports camp, being held at an outdoor bounds activity centre in an old boarding school in the Welsh mountains. A high wooden wall surrounded the building and its massive grounds, so it was safe and secluded.

It was the afternoon of Day One and, so far, things were shaping up well. Arjun and Kev were sharing a room in a one-storey wooden unit. The food was pretty decent and the timetable looked awesome.

At the moment they were in the middle of a game of baseball; later on they'd be going for a ride on mountain bikes through the local rocky terrain.

A man named Marcus and a woman called Carol were the leaders at the camp and they seemed like a good laugh. They looked about twenty or twenty-one.

They'd told everyone that some other leaders would be joining them in a couple of days. The leaders' accommodation was housed in a block on the opposite side of the canteen from the kids' blocks.

'Check this out!' shouted Kev, giving the ball a thunderous whack and sending it flying to the far reaches of the field.

As Kev ran past first base, Arjun hared after the ball. They might be friends, but when it came to sport, they were both seriously competitive.

*****

There was a good atmosphere in the canteen that night. After baseball, the mountain biking had been great.

'The only bad thing about this camp is that we had to hand in our mobile phones,' said a girl called Maya, who had bleached blonde hair and a nose ring.

'Totally,' nodded Arjun. 'I can't go to bed unless I've spent at least two hours playing games.'

This drew a laugh from everyone except for a shaggy-haired boy called Mike, who had so far kept himself to himself. Whenever he could, he went back to his dorm.

'OK,' announced Carol, standing up when the meal was over. 'In case of an emergency, you'll hear this sound.'

She pulled a small klaxon out of her pocket and gave it a squeeze. A loud honk, like a foghorn, filled the air.

'Whenever you hear that noise,' continued Marcus, 'you need to get inside this canteen as quickly as possible. We'll be practising tomorrow, so listen out for it.'

Arjun yawned. Kev grinned and gave him a playful punch on the arm.

'This is no joke,' said Carol, her laid-back expression suddenly turning hard.

'Carol's right,' nodded Marcus, looking equally severe. 'This is deadly serious.'

Kev's smile vanished and for a few seconds a sour atmosphere hung in the air, but then Marcus and Carol were smiling again and announcing that hot chocolate

would be served in half an hour, after some games in the main hall.

Everyone piled out of the canteen, but when Arjun looked back he saw Marcus and Carol locked in heavy conversation.

For some reason, something about the way they were huddled together sent an icy twist of unease snaking down his spine.

CHAPTER 2

Next morning, Arjun and Kev woke up
before anyone else. The grass outside their
dorm was wet and glistening.

'Let's go and explore,' said Arjun.

They followed a wide stone path that led
beyond the dorms and the canteen. Soon
they were tramping through a muddy field

and into a wood on the south side of the site.

'Check that out!' said Kev, pointing up to a high-wire course strung out between trees, with bridges, climbs and a zip wire.

'I hope we get to go on that today,' said Arjun.

When they emerged from the wood they found themselves on a narrow track that curved first left, and then right. It ended when they reached the high wooden perimeter fence.

'That's pretty good for stopping anyone getting into the camp,' mused Arjun, staring up at the fence.

'Maybe it's to stop us getting out!' grinned Kev, doing his best 'deranged monster attack' impression.

'Get off!' laughed Arjun, pushing him away.

'I'm going to climb it,' said Kev, grabbing on to the wood and trying to pull himself up. He slipped straight back down. He tried again, but the same thing happened.

'It's got anti-climb paint,' said a voice. 'You won't get over it.'

The boys spun round and saw Marcus, standing and staring at them.

'We weren't really going to climb it,' said Arjun.

'You shouldn't have come here without informing us,' said Marcus curtly. 'You need to head back. Everyone else is getting up and there's loads to do.'

No one said anything on the walk to the canteen, where the others were already eating breakfast.

Carol raised an eyebrow at Marcus. He nodded.

Arjun glanced at Kev and frowned.

*****

The day's activities were brilliant. In the morning they did quad biking and archery. After lunch they worked on building bridges across a small river, and canoeing.

After the canoeing there'd been a huge water fight, led by Arjun and Kev.

Mike had refused to get involved. He sat with his back to everyone, some way away from the others. Marcus and Carol though were on top form, joining in with all of the activities, including the water fight.

The only annoying thing about the day was the klaxon alerts.

'Don't you think we know the drill by now?' complained Maya in the canteen, when they'd gathered there after the fourth klaxon roar.

'We can't practise it enough!' snapped Carol. 'It could mean the difference between life and death.'

*****

After supper there was a treasure hunt in the woods. Arjun and Kev's team won, which pleased them ever so slightly.

'You were just lucky!' grinned Maya.

'Marcus and Carol are weird,' said Arjun, when they were back in their dorm.

'I know,' replied Kev. 'One minute they're all fun and games, the next they go all psycho about the emergency canteen meetings.'

'What do you think is up with them?' asked Arjun.

'I'm not sure,' shivered Kev. 'I'm really enjoying the activities, but there's something about those two that creeps me out a bit.'

'I know what you mean,' nodded Arjun.

They got into their beds.

Even though they were tired, it took them a long time to get to sleep.

CHAPTER 3

The following morning, Arjun was woken up at about 6 a.m. by voices near the dorm.

He lifted the curtain a fraction and saw Marcus and Carol waving a welcome to a car as it pulled up next to the canteen.

A young man and a woman got out. It was then all hugs and hellos.

Marcus and Carol led the new arrivals in the direction of the leaders' block.

Arjun was about to roll over and go back to sleep when a thought struck him. Where were the new people's bags? They didn't seem to have any with them. If they did, they'd surely take them out of the car when they got here.

Wasn't that a bit strange?

Arjun decided that they must have left their stuff in the car, and forgot about it.

*****

The new leaders were called Simon and Bev.

Like Marcus and Carol, they were really great fun during the activities, but became very serious when practising the emergency klaxon alerts. They did three the following morning.

The day's activities were rope climbing, the high wire course, a ground obstacle track and making shelters in the woods with branches and ropes.

They all ate supper in the shelters, Marcus and Carol cooking the food on little camping stoves.

'As well as Bev and Simon, some other leaders will be joining us soon,' announced Carol, 'and when we're complete the real fun will begin!'

'It's going to be amazing!' agreed Marcus with a wide grin.

'What do you think *real fun* will involve?' whispered Arjun.

Kev shrugged his shoulders.

*****

After a late night sports quiz, all of the kids stayed up chatting for a while, apart from Mike who slunk off to his room.

Finally everyone turned in for the night. Arjun and Kev went to their dorm. They turned off the light.

They waited.

When they saw the last of the other dorm lights go off, they snuck out into the night.

'There's definitely something weird about Marcus and Carol,' Arjun had observed that afternoon, 'and now Simon and Bev are here and they're really similar. Something weird is going on here and I think we should investigate.'

Kev had immediately agreed.

They kept low and crept past the other kids' dorms, following the path round the canteen. The leaders' block stood there in the darkness, its lights marking the place out like a lighthouse.

On they stole, until they reached the side of the building. They passed a couple of dorms, cupped their hands against the glass and looked in.

The beds inside had clearly been slept in, but there were no clothes, no shoes and no bags to be seen.

'Maybe everything's packed away in the cupboards,' whispered Kev.

'No one puts *everything* away,' hissed Arjun, 'not even my mum, and she's the tidiest person in the world.'

The noise of people chatting wafted through the air. They could hear individual voices – Marcus's, Carol's and Bev's – but they didn't sound like their normal voices. They were lower, with a sort of growling tone.

Kev shot Arjun a quick glance, his face showing his fear.

Arjun put a finger on his lips and edged forward.

They reached the room where the voices were coming from. A large blind covered the window, but there was a strip of window at the side that was wide enough for the boys to see in.

And what they saw chilled them to the marrow.

Their four leaders were sitting in the room talking.

At least, it *was* them, but at the same time it wasn't.

Because each of the four figures looked like un-dead versions of themselves.

Chapter 4

Kev was about to let out a scream, but Arjun covered his mouth and whispered. 'Move!'

As quietly as they could, they stepped away from the block, circled the canteen and raced back to their dorm, their hearts beating furiously.

Instead of going in, they stood behind the dorm block.

'Did you see what I saw back there?' asked Kev, shaking with fear.

'They looked like skeletons with rotten flesh sticking to them,' replied Arjun, goose-bumps covering his arms and legs.

'It was horrible. It must have been Marcus, Carol, Simon and Bev – but zombie versions of them. And don't forget what they said. There are going to be more joining them soon.'

'Yeah,' nodded Kev, his face an oval of pale anxiety, 'they said when the others arrive they'll be *complete*, whatever that means.'

'They looked disgusting,' said Arjun, 'and that was through a blind. Can you imagine what they look like close-up?'

'What are we going to do?' asked Kev.

'We haven't got our phones and the perimeter wall is un-climbable,' said Arjun grimly. 'None of this can be a coincidence.'

'Do you think they'll attack us in our beds?' asked a petrified Kev.

'I've no idea, but I don't want to find out.'

'Shall we tell everyone else?'

'Not yet. We'd scare the life out of them.'

'So what do you suggest?'

'I suggest we take our sleeping bags and spend the night somewhere else.'

'OK. But where?'

'Follow me,' said Arjun. They nipped inside their dorm, grabbed their sleeping bags and set out.

Hurrying towards the south-side woods, they both looked over their shoulders every few seconds, terrified of what they might see behind them. But no one was following them.

Ten minutes later, they were climbing the steps carved into a giant oak tree up towards the high wires. At the top of the steps was a square platform.

'This is where we spend the night,' said Arjun. 'We're well off the ground here. We have a decent view, so we'll know straight away if they come anywhere near us.'

'Do you think they will?' asked Kev.

Arjun shrugged his shoulders.

'Let's get through the night first and see if they're still those creatures in the morning. If they are, all of the other kids will see them and join us in a fight against them if necessary.'

'They looked horrific!' shivered Kev.

They climbed into their sleeping bags. There was just enough room for them to rest their backs against the side of the platform. Although it was cold, it was summer-night cold, so it was bearable.

'We'll take it in turns to stay awake,' said Arjun. 'I'll go first.'

'Are you sure you'll be able to?' asked Kev, stifling a big yawn.

'Absolutely,' nodded Arjun, checking his watch. 'It's 11.30 p.m. now. I'll wake you at 1.30.'

'Fine,' nodded Kev.

He got as comfortable as he could and within a few minutes he was fast asleep.

Arjun kept his eyes on the ground, searching for any sign of an approach. But the woods were empty.

Ten minutes after midnight, he felt his eyelids drooping. He forced them open. They tried to close again.

He started going over the name of everyone he knew in his school, in a bid not to fall asleep.

When he'd done this, he tried to picture the front door and number of every house on his street. But by 12.50 a.m. he lost the fight, his head drooped and sleep engulfed him.

*****

He was woken by a throaty whisper. Someone was calling his name.

His eyes snapped open and, in horror, he saw four repugnant zombies, their flesh sliding around on their bones, their eyes deep red and fiery.

They were all climbing the wooden steps up to the platform.

Arjun screamed and kicked Kev awake.

CHAPTER 5

'Don't move!' hissed the first zombie, only a few rungs below the platform.

Its voice was the same as Marcus's, but far lower, with that horrible growling pitch.

'HELP!' screamed Kev, his eyes enormous, staring in total shock at the four hideous creatures hurrying up the oak steps.

Now that Kev and Arjun could see them properly, reflected in the moonlight, they looked truly appalling.

Their skeletons were covered with rotting scraps of flesh that hung like melting cheese on a pizza. Their red eyes sat in deep and curved eye sockets.

But Kev and Arjun were much too far away from the dorms for anyone to hear Kev's cry for help.

In an instant he and Arjun were out of their sleeping bags and racing along a rickety wooden bridge high in the trees.

'STOP RUNNING!' shouted zombie Carol, but the sound of her voice alone was enough to keep the boys running in terror. Stumbling across a mesh of wires, Kev almost fell over, but Arjun pulled him up by his shirtsleeve.

The zombies were all moaning and hissing as they pursued the boys. Arjun was just a step in front of Kev.

'QUICK!' yelled Kev, as he and Arjun turned a corner and raced up several mini steps and through a wire tunnel with a tarpaulin over the top.

With each step the zombies were gaining on them. The boys tried desperately not to think about what the hideous beasts would do to them if they caught them.

'YOU WON'T GET AWAY!' shrieked zombie Bev.

Arjun and Kev rounded another corner and then spied the zip wire up ahead. This was an incredibly long length of wire that sloped down for at least a hundred metres. There was a line of leather handles fixed to its top.

Arjun grabbed the first one and instantly went speeding down the wire.

Kev was right behind him and grabbed the second handle. As he let himself go, he thought about the other handles. He went to grab them as well, but he was too late. He'd missed them.

So when the boys looked back, they saw zombie Marcus grasp the next handle with his rotting hands, let out a blood-curdling scream and come zooming down after them.

Chapter 6

It took a few minutes for all of the zombies to hit the ground at the bottom of the zip wire.

They gazed at each other in confusion, their rotting faces looking this way and that.

'Where are they?' demanded zombie Carol, her voice throaty and menacing.

'I can't see them anywhere,' snarled zombie Simon.

'OK,' declared zombie Marcus. 'Let's split up. Each take a direction and fan out. They can't have gone far.'

'Shout out if you find them!' commanded zombie Carol.

They shook each other's grotesque hands and set off.

In a small covered hole in the ground lay Arjun and Kev, shivering. They'd spotted it the second they'd landed and had jumped in, pulling some branches over themselves before zombie Marcus had reached the end of the zip wire.

*****

They waited for what felt like five hours, but was in fact only half an hour.

Arjun stood on tiptoes and moved a couple of branches to one side, so he could see out. A shadowy mist was rolling just above the ground.

Wherever he looked, he couldn't see any sign of the zombies.

Silently, Arjun nodded and climbed out of the hole. Kev scrambled out a few seconds later.

'Do you think there's anyone we can go to for help?' asked Kev. 'A local farm or something?'

'You saw that wooden fence when we drove in. It stretches round every inch of this place. And remember the anti-climb paint? It's a non-starter.'

'What about that gate we drove through when we got here?'

'It slammed shut when we were in. There's no way out.'

'Well, if there are more of them coming, shouldn't we get everyone up and fight them now?'

Arjun put his head to one side, lost in thought.

'One part of me wants to, but the other part says that doing that would be a complete disaster. If we get everyone up, in the pandemonium and terror, we'll all be easy targets.

'I say we try and get through this night, get as much info as we can about their plans, and then attack them.'

Kev sighed deeply.

'Are we going back to the dorm, then?'

Arjun nodded.

Kevin's anxious expression became more extreme.

*****

Through the mist they crept, their bodies in a state of high anxiety. Every twig snapping, every crunch under foot making them jump.

They snuck into their room and immediately set to work. They pushed the big wardrobe against the door and, behind this, they shoved the two chairs and their suitcases.

They stood with their bodies pressed against this makeshift barrier, ready to defend themselves.

Neither of them had ever been so tense. Each second dragged by as if it was tied to an enormous lead weight. The clock reached 3, then 4, then 5 and 6.

At 6.45 a.m. they were so focussed on the door that they didn't hear the whistling sound outside.

Which is why they were totally unprepared for something crashing through one of the windows and smashing it into thousands of pieces.

Chapter 7

Kev screamed, a piercing shriek, but Arjun grabbed him.

'It's not them!' cried Arjun, 'It's Maya.'

And he was right.

A terribly guilty-looking Maya was standing outside, staring at the large hole in the window.

The boys looked down at the floor, where an orange football now stood. That's what had broken the glass.

'I am SO sorry,' said Maya, 'Me and Kirsty woke up early and fancied a kick about.'

'It's … it's … fine,' Arjun managed to reply. 'We were expecting someone else.'

Maya frowned. 'What do you mean?' she asked.

'Long story,' said Arjun.

'What's going on over there?'

It was Carol's voice. Her real voice, not the horrible zombie crackle. Through the window Arjun and Kev could see Carol walking over to Maya and Kirsty.

Carol had completely returned to her normal self. Gone was all sign of flesh and bone, and she was behaving as if nothing had happened in the night.

Maya explained the football/broken window situation.

'Not a great way to start the day,' smiled Carol, 'but also not the end of the world. I'll get a dustpan and brush. Don't anyone go near the glass.'

Maya disappeared and a few seconds later she tried the handle of Arjun and Kev's room. The door didn't budge. The boys quickly pulled the wardrobe and chairs to one side.

'Did you barricade yourselves in here?' she asked, walking in and checking out the glass fragments. 'And what did you mean when you said "it's not *them*"?'

'We were just having a laugh,' said Arjun. 'You know, playing a mad game.'

Maya gave him a funny look, but just then Carol reappeared, carrying a dustpan and brush.

'Are you two boys OK?' she asked Arjun and Kev kindly.

They recoiled in horror. This was a creature who had been pursuing them for some terrifying purpose just a few hours ago.

Was it possible that *this* Carol didn't know about zombie Carol? Was it possible that she didn't remember the hideous change that had come over her in the night?

Or was she just very good at *pretending*, somehow?

Or had Arjun and Kev imagined the whole thing?

Carol swept up the glass and said she'd get Bev to fix it as soon as possible – Bev was apparently very handy.

*****

Arjun and Kev kept a close eye on all of the leaders that day, but there wasn't even the tiniest chink in their human armour to reveal their zombie selves.

It made the boys think again that they might have imagined the whole thing.

After a morning's swimming in a lake, and a session of cross-country running, everyone had a picnic lunch in one of the big fields.

Arjun needed the toilet and said he'd quickly nip back to the dorms. He was halfway there when he spotted Marcus and Carol deep in conversation, leaning against a wall.

In silence he crept behind the wall and stopped to eavesdrop on them.

'The others will be here soon,' Marcus was saying.

'They're better get here quickly,' replied Carol. 'The four of us already here will meet at the stone circle at midnight and plan the next stage.'

'And then when the others arrive, we'll unleash ourselves,' said Marcus.

They both laughed.

And Arjun could hear a low, growly tone somewhere inside those laughs.

CHAPTER 8

'What was that about midnight?' asked
Maya, strolling over to Arjun and Kev, who
were sitting on a large rock, talking about
the conversation Arjun had overheard.

It was a couple of hours later and an
abseiling activity had just finished.

'We were talking about the possibility of a midnight feast,' said Kev quickly.

'Tonight?' asked Maya.

'Maybe,' replied Arjun. 'We'll see how things pan out.'

'Did either of you hear weird noises in the night?' asked Maya, sitting down next to them.

'What kind of noises?' asked Kev.

'It was kind of like low growling, a bit like wolves,' answered Maya. 'Although I doubt there any wolves hanging out round here.'

'Nah,' said Arjun, 'didn't hear anything until you kicked our window in.'

Maya laughed.

Arjun and Kev didn't.

*****

There were no signs of any other leaders arriving that day. After an afternoon game of very muddy rugby, everyone went to grab showers before supper.

Arjun and Kev found an old map of the site in the canteen. The stone circle Marcus and Carol had talked about was located in a clearing in the woods on the north side of the estate.

'If the others don't arrive today, maybe we'll have a window of time to stop whatever it is they're planning,' said Kev.

Arjun nodded. 'Step one is to spy on them at the stone circle tonight.'

*****

They set out at 11.15 p.m., carrying the site map and a torch. The plan was to get there, hide themselves, and glean as much information as they could.

Once they knew what the four zombie leaders were really up to, they'd tell all of the other kids on the site and form a small army. They had to keep at least one step ahead of the zombies.

The trees on the north side were more densely packed than the ones they'd navigated through before, and they both picked up scratches on their faces as they made their way forwards.

After struggling through the wood they emerged on the other side in a clearing. In the centre of the clearing was a large bonfire, crackling and hissing, the wooden logs giving off an orangey-red glow.

'Right,' said Arjun. 'Let's hide behind that bush over there. They won't know we're here.'

'Oh I think we will,' said a terrifying voice.

Arjun and Tom looked around them in horror, as ten zombies stepped out from behind the trees.

CHAPTER 9

'I guess the others *did* make it here,' gulped Kev, as the zombies advanced slowly towards the boys, their grotesque, slippery faces plastered with jagged, toothed smiles.

Arjun and Kev had never moved so fast. They just turned on their heels and ran.

The path they'd used to arrive was blocked by zombie Carol, who was holding out her arms to catch them.

They turned to their left and saw the smallest zombie in their way. Rushing at it, Arjun used his shoulder to barge it out of the way.

It screamed in fury as it reeled backwards, allowing the boys a tiny gap to run through.

And run they did.

Sprinting as fast as they'd ever run, they tore through a further stretch of the wood, the branches attacking them with every step.

Arjun took a quick look round and his heart lurched violently when he saw that the zombies weren't running after them: instead, they were floating through the air.

And fast.

Over mud and stones and twigs the boys ran, and as they hurtled forwards they suddenly caught sight of the wooden perimeter wall.

They rushed towards it and tried to jump onto it, but the anti-climb paint repelled them.

They stood with their backs against the wall as the ten zombies floated to the ground and stood in a line, less than six feet away.

'Well, well, well,' growled zombie Marcus, as he and zombie Carol took a further step towards them. 'Did you really think you'd be able to get to the stone circle before us and spy on us? We're a bit too clever to fall into that trap.'

The boys said nothing. Their bodies were shaking with terror.

'B … b … but why are you here?' Arjun finally managed to stutter. 'What have we done to you?'

Zombie Carol threw back her bony skull and let out a high-pitched cackle.

'Don't pretend you don't know!' she snarled. 'Last summer the ten of us and a leader called Lauren, who hasn't made it here yet, arrived at this camp as leaders. But before we could even meet anyone or start the summer camp, our hut was set on fire and we all burned to death!'

'Yeah!' cried zombie Marcus. 'Nobody came to our rescue. We were left there to die.'

'What's that got to do with us?' asked Kev.

'Lots of you here will have been here last summer and lots of you will have come again this year. That makes lots of you partly responsible for our deaths!' roared zombie Carol.

'None of you came to help us when we screamed!' snapped zombie Marcus.

'We rose from our ashes and have perfected the art of looking human,' said zombie Carol. 'No one outside this camp knows anything about our mission!'

'And we all gave different names on our application forms for this camp, so no one would know we were the same people from last year!' added zombie Bev, with a repulsive grin.

'Are those klaxon alerts connected to this?' asked Arjun anxiously.

'Of course,' nodded zombie Simon. 'We want to make sure we can summon you all to the canteen at any time of day or night, so that we can get rid of you in one go! But now it looks like we may have to destroy you two a little bit earlier than the others!'

'But *we* weren't here last year,' protested Kev in terror.

'Who cares!' snapped zombie Carol. 'We're going to dispose of the lot of you. 1972 was the year we lost our lives. 1973 will be the year you lose yours! Now we're all here, there's nothing stopping us. Our revenge will be complete!'

'What do you mean, *1973*?' said Kev.

'This year!' hissed zombie Carol. '1973.'

'But this year *isn't* 1973,' said Arjun, 'it's 2023. It's fifty one years after you say you died.'

There were gasps of shock from the other zombies.

'YOU LIE!' screeched zombie Carol. 'And now you will pay for it.'

She raised her hand in the air and brought it crashing down towards Arjun's skull.

CHAPTER 10

'STOP!' cried zombie Simon, grasping zombie Carol's hand a split-second before it made contact with Arjun's head.

'RELEASE ME!' screamed zombie Carol. 'THIS IS AN UNTRUTH SPREAD BY THESE DISGUSTING HUMAN KILLERS!'

'She's right!' shouted zombie Marcus. 'This is the only reason why we all brought ourselves back from the dead; to exact revenge on our killers.'

'But if they're telling the truth, then they're not our killers,' said zombie Simon.

'It is the truth,' said Arjun.

'Maybe it is that far in the future,' murmured zombie Bev. 'After all, I did see that Mike boy holding a weird gadget. Once I spotted him speaking into it, and another time I saw moving pictures on its screen.'

Suddenly it hit Arjun and Kev why Mike spent so much time alone. He'd sneaked in his mobile.

'It's called a mobile phone!' said Kev eagerly, and then he thought of his watch. 'Look,' he said, showing it to zombie Simon.

'It says the current year is 2023 right here. We're not lying.'

Zombie Simon gazed at the watch for a few moments.

'You've miscalculated badly!' he fumed venomously at zombies Marcus and Carol. 'You've taken us fifty years into the future!'

'They're LYING!' screamed zombie Carol desperately.

'Getting the date wrong is a death sentence!' wailed zombie Bev. 'You all know that!'

At that moment the zombies started shaking from side-to-side, the patches of flesh on their bones sliding around. They started groaning and hissing.

Arjun and Kev took a horrified step backwards.

The skin was now sliding off the zombies' bodies, falling onto the ground in gruesome clumps.

'We're dying again!' screeched zombie Bev, as the last flaps of skin slid off her body. There were now ten skeletons shaking and shivering in the cold night air.

Then, with a series of strange popping sounds, the bones fell apart and dropped clattering onto the ground. They rolled about for a few seconds and then came to a stop.

The boys stood there for the next few minutes, completely speechless.

Finally Kev mustered the energy to say something.

'No one is going to believe us, are they?' he whispered, staring at the carpet of scattered, lifeless bones.

'Probably not,' replied Arjun, 'but at least all of this stuff on the ground is evidence. It will be very hard for anyone to explain away all of this.'

'Let's head back,' said Kev. 'We'd better wake everyone up and try to convince them about everything we've seen.'

'I agree,' nodded Arjun.

But as they turned to leave, they heard a crackly, whispered cry.

'It's me, zombie Lauren,' hissed the voice at the boys. 'I just got here. I was the eleventh leader. I heard what you said, but I don't believe a word of it. I KNOW it's 1973 and I WILL take my revenge!'

Arjun and Kev looked at each other in horror and began sprinting as fast as they could in the direction of the dorms.

As they neared the dorms, zombie Lauren saw a poster dated July 26 2023. She screamed in horror and, just like the others, her skin started melting.

Before long she was just a collection of bones.

'We have to get to Mike as quickly as possible,' panted Arjun. 'We need to get the police here and I think we're going to need his phone!'

More great Toxic reads

Action-packed adventure stories featuring jungles, swamps, deserted islands, robots, space travel, zombies, computer viruses and monsters from the deep.

How many have you read?

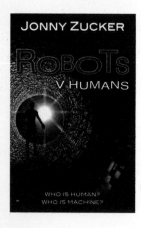

Robots v Humans

by Jonny Zucker

Nico finds himself with five other kids – all his age. None of them can remember anything from their past. Then they are told that three of them are human and the other three are robots. Can Nico find out who is human and who are the robots?

78

VIRUS 21

by Jonny Zucker

A new computer virus is rapidly spreading throughout the world. It is infecting everything, closing down hospitals, airports and even the internet. Can Troy and Macy find the hackers before the whole world shuts down?

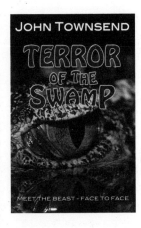

TERROR OF THE SWAMP

by John Townsend

Ex-SAS explorer Baron and his son Greg have been sent to the African jungle to find a lost TV crew. It's a search that brings them face to face with the mysterious ancient terrors of the swamp – and it could cost them their lives.

Jonny Zucker has been a teacher, musician, stand-up comedian and footballer, but now he is best known as one of the most popular authors for children. So far he has written over 100 books.

Jonny also plays in a band and has done over 60 gigs as a stand-up comedian, reaching the London Region Final of the BBC New Comedy awards.

He still dreams of being a professional footballer.